First Bride
By Anthony Uyl

Devoted Publishing
Woodstock, Ontario, 2017

First Bride
By Anthony Uyl

What kind of stories do you have?
Let us know!

Visit our website: www.devotedpublishing.com
Contact us at: devotedpub@hotmail.com
Visit us on Facebook: @DevotedPublishing

Published in Woodstock, Ontario, Canada 2017

For bulk theatrical rates, please contact us at the above email address.

ISBN: 978-1-77356-094-6

Act 1

INT. - TEMPLE FOYER – NIGHT

The temple is an old church that is now being used by a coven of witches. The foyer is open and has two doors on each side for offices.

INT. - OFFICE – NIGHT

PAMELA is in one of the offices behind a desk on the phone. She is wearing a set of black robes.

PAMELA:
Yes tonight will be a great night, we've been preparing for this for a long time.

Mumbling coming from phone.

PAMELA:
The moon and stars are in their proper positions tonight, if we don't do it tonight then all our preparations over the years will be for nothing.

Mumbling coming from phone.

PAMELA:
I'm glad you're supporting us in this. Have you done your part?

Mumbling coming from phone.

PAMELA:
Once the ritual is complete I'm sure she'll want to head down there and meet up with him.

Mumbling coming from phone.

PAMELA:
Well I have to go, someone is coming in.

INT. - FOYER – NIGHT

JUDITH walks into the foyer and approaches the office.

JUDITH:
Pamela?

Pamela comes out of the office in the foyer.

PAMELA:
Yes Judith, I'm so glad you could come tonight.

JUDITH:
It was required, I would hate to disappoint my mistress.

PAMELA:
And you haven't. Go get in your robes and we'll meet you in the chapel.

First Bride
>   JUDITH:
Yes, my mistress.

>   *Judith heads down towards the chapel but turns before entering, she goes into another room. She emerges a few seconds later wearing red robes. More LADIES begin to enter in to the foyer, some are wearing the red robes, others are not.*

>   PAMELA:
My sisters, welcome to this spectacular night.

>   *One of the ladies wearing robes approaches Pamela and kisses her on the lips.*

>   PAMELA:
Thank you sister, go and prepare for the ritual.

>   KISSING SISTER:
Yes, mistress.

>   *The ladies continue to come into the foyer, some stop and shake or hug Pamela but they all manage to get into the chapel. Pamela enters the chapel.*

INT. - CHAPEL – NIGHT

>   *The chapel is decorated in a red tones. There are no pews and red banners hand down from the ceiling. The banners have the female circle and arrow on top of the male circle and cross symbol. There is a stage at the front.*

>   PAMELA:
Welcome sisters, tonight is a glorious night that we have been preparing for for many years. Tonight we see the fruits of our hard work.

>   *The ladies cheer. Pamela walks up to the stage. On the stage are two cages one holding the woman who becomes LILITH and a SACRIFICIAL MAN who is wearing a black tux.*

>   LILITH:
Please let us go, we haven't done anything.

>   *Pamela ignores her.*

>   SACRIFICIAL MAN:
We'll do anything, pay anything.

>   PAMELA:
There is nothing you have that I want.

>   LILITH:
Please, I beg you. I have family that will look for me.

>   PAMELA:
>   *(smiles evilly)*
Not anymore they won't.

>   LILITH:
>   *(cries)*
What? What is that supposed to mean?

>   PAMELA:
Ladies, prepare the sacrifices.

The ladies cheer and five of them come up on stage. They unlock both cages. Three women drag the man, who fights back, to a set of chains hanging from the ceiling and bind him in them. The woman they tie to a stone altar in the middle of the stage. Pamela walks behind the altar and grabs a knife.

PAMELA:
(in Latin)
Lilith we call to you to come to us.

WOMEN:
(in Latin)
Yes, Lilith come.

PAMELA:
(in Latin)
We offer up this sacrifice to you, to honor you.

Pamela stabs the sacrificial man. Blood pours out of the wound and the man coughs up some blood. He tries to keep his eyes open for a few seconds then dies.

PAMELA:
(in Latin)
We have offered you a worthy sacrifice, now we offer you one more to honor what you are to do.

WOMEN:
(in Latin)
Yes, Lilith come.

INSERT – LILITH'S EYES

Lilith's eyes suddenly open up and a red light is seen coming from them.

BACK TO CHAPEL

Pamela goes to stab Lilith but she breaks the chains holding her down and grabs the knife out of Pamela's hand.

PAMELA:
How did you do that?

LILITH:
Behold child I have come.

PAMELA:
You were supposed to come into me.

LILITH:
I will come into whom I choose.

Lilith stabs Pamela. Pamela falls over the altar and blood starts to pour down the sides of the altar. Pamela dies. The women scream. They rush to exit the chapel but Lilith raises her hand and the doors close. The women cannot get out.

JUDITH:
Please don't hurt us.

LILITH:
Yes you will all do very well.

Lilith leaps off the stage and rips out the heart of one of the women. She begins slashing and cutting the women apart. Judith hides beneath one of the bodies gasping for breath. Lilith walks past her then suddenly lifts Judith into the air.

First Bride
JUDITH:
Please, I can serve you.

LILITH:
You already have.

JUDITH:
I can help you get to him.

LILITH:
I have no need of your help.

JUDITH:
(cries)
Please let me live.

LILITH:
You are not worthy of life.

Lilith stabs Judith. Lilith drops Judith to the floor then walks out of the chapel doors that open automatically for her.

EXT. - ROAD – NIGHT

Lilith is walking down a gravel road which intersects with a paved highway. She walks onto the highway unafraid. A horn is heard blaring and Lilith turns to stare right into a oncoming cars headlights.

ANGRY DRIVER:
Get out of the way you crazy bitch.

The car swerves around her. Lilith raises up her hand and the four tires on the car all pop. The car rolls into the ditch. Lilith walks up to the overturned car.

ANGRY DRIVER:
What the? How did you do that?

LILITH:
You'd be surprised at what I can do bitch.

ANGRY DRIVER:
You're crazy.

LILITH:
Maybe a little.

Lilith stabs the man with the knife in the head. She leaves the knife sticking out of the mans head as she walks away.

INT. - VATICAN CLASSROOM – DAY

The classroom is set up like a typical classroom. At the front of the room is BROTHER ANDREWS who is teaching the ten students who are in the class. JEREMIAH and JAMES are in the back of the room. The men and women are sll dressed in robes.

BROTHER ANDREWS:
We are the Inquisition, we exist to purge the world of evil brought on to us by the sin of man.

JAMES:
(to Jeremiah)
Can you believe this? I'd rather be outside enjoying the sunshine.

JEREMIAH:
(to James)
Yeah, me too.

BROTHER ANDREWS:
You have been trained to fight and to use your minds when dealing with the supernatural. Always remember your tenants of faith and you will never go wrong in dealing with them.

JAMES:
(to Jeremiah)
What're your plans for the weekend?

JEREMIAH:
(to James)
Well seeing as we actually have a weekend off, I'm going to relax and spend some time away from here.

JAMES:
(to Jeremiah)
Yeah I hear ya.

BROTHER ANDREWS:
Brothers James and Jeremiah, do you have anything to add to the class?

JAMES:
No, brother we do not.

BROTHER ANDREWS:
And what were you talking about that could not wait till after class?

JAMES:
Nothing important, brother, I apologize.

BROTHER ANDRES:
Don't let it happen again.

JAMES:
Yes brother.

REBECCA looks back at Jeremiah and smiles. Jeremiah smiles back.

BROTHER ANDREWS:
That ends our class for today. Have a good weekend off and we'll see you all back Monday morning after chores and prayer.

WHOLE CLASS:
Amen, brother.

INT. - HALLWAY – DAY

The class starts to empty out and Jeremiah and James are walking together casually.

JAMES:
So when were you planning on heading out?

JEREMIAH:
As soon as I can get out of these.

JAMES:
You want to hang out together?

JEREMIAH:
I have no interest in getting drunk with you.

JAMES:
Oh, come on, it'll be fun.

JEREMIAH:
That's what you said last time and we ended up doing penance for it.

JAMES:
And I apologized for that. You won't reconsider?

JEREMIAH:
Definitely not.

JAMES:
Fine, you used to be more fun than this.
(laughs)

JEREMIAH:
Got to grow up sometime.

JAMES:
Me? Nah, not right now.

JEREMIAH:
See you later.

JAMES:
Later, man.

Rebecca walks quietly up to Jeremiah and surprises him.

REBECCA:
Hey.

JEREMIAH:
Hey.

REBECCA:
Couldn't help but overhear that you're heading out of here for the evening.

JEREMIAH:
Yeah.

REBECCA:
You want some company?

JEREMIAH:
I already turned James down.

REBECCA:
Yes, well, he's getting drunk I wasn't suggesting that.

JEREMIAH:
Then what do you want to do?

REBECCA:
I was thinking of getting some dinner at a pasta place not to far from here.

JEREMIAH:
Like a date?

REBECCA:
Well, I don't know if...

JEREMIAH:
I just got out of a pretty serious relationship with my ex, I'm not sure I'm up to dating yet.

REBECCA:
Then just as friends.

JEREMIAH:
So, we're friends now?

REBECCA:
Sure.

JEREMIAH:
Alright, I'll meet you there.

REBECCA:
Great.

INT. - PASTA RESTAURANT – NIGHT

Rebecca is waiting for Jeremiah to show up. She is fidgeting quite a bit and constantly looking at her watch. After a few seconds Jeremiah comes in rushed. He looks around and sees her sitting at a table and comes and sits down.

JEREMIAH:
Were you waiting long?

REBECCA:
No, it's fine.

JEREMIAH:
Sorry, I had to turn down James again.

REBECCA:
You guys are pretty good friends aren't you?

JEREMIAH:
Yeah, we are. Even though he gets me into trouble.

REBECCA:
I think you enjoy it.

JEREMIAH:
Maybe a little.

The WAITER comes up.

WAITER:
So what can I get you?

JEREMIAH:
I'll have the sausage alfredo.

REBECCA:
So will I.

WAITER:
Very good.

REBECCA:
So what made you become an infamous inquisitor?

JEREMIAH:
Well, I used to work at a museum back in the States as a security guard. An egyptologist we had working there was careless and managed to raise some of the dead we had there. I and a girl I ended up dating ended up fighting them off and re-killing the dead. The museum was destroyed and the Inquisition came and offered me a job.

REBECCA:
Sounds pretty intense.

JEREMIAH:
Scared the shit right out of me.

REBECCA:
So what about this girl?

JEREMIAH:
Her name was Hanna. We dated for a little bit after that night but it didn't last. She was to traumatized by the experience and needed to much help.

REBECCA:
I see.

JEREMIAH:
What about you? How'd you get recruited?

REBECCA:
Well, my sister was dating this guy and another guy, Eric, wanted her as well. Eric was a practicing warlock and ended up putting a curse on Amy's boyfriend. The curse was more than he was expecting and Amy's boyfriend, Charlie, ended up becoming possessed. Charlie, took my sister and started to make her work corners and take drugs. He killed Eric and started to come after my family. I took it upon myself to do something. So I found an exorcism and sent the spirit back to where it came from.

JEREMIAH:
What happened to your sister?

REBECCA:
She went into rehab, but still needs a lot of help. She's been diagnosed with post traumatic stress disorder and is constantly reliving the things Charlie made her do.

JEREMIAH:
That's sad, I'm so sorry.

REBECCA:
Yeah, but we all got through it alive, and that's what matters.

JEREMIAH:
True.

INT. - SUBURBAN HOME – NIGHT

SUSAN is doing the dishes when TOM her husband stumbles through the front door.

TOM:
Susie, are you here?

SUSAN:
Yes, dear I'm here.

TOM:
You're not out whoring yourself out again are you?

SUSAN:
I have never done that to you.

TOM:
Well those aren't my damn kids upstairs.

SUSAN:
Yes, they are Tom. Don't you remember getting the blood work done?

TOM:
The doctor lied to us, you're sleeping with him too.

SUSAN:
No, I'm not.

TOM:
Yeah you are you slut.

SUSAN:
(cries)
Look, just go get some sleep, please.

Tom slaps Susan.

TOM:
Don't tell me what to do you bitch.

SUSAN:
I'm sorry, I didn't mean to.

TOM:
Then why did you?

SUSAN:
I just think you could use some sleep.

Susan looks out the window and Lilith walks confidently past the window facing the sidewalk. Lilith stops and looks at her. Susan looks at her with a confused look on her face.

TOM:
I don't need nothin', especially since you think I do.

SUSAN:
Just go upstairs I have to finish the housework.

TOM:
Fine, but I want you up there in five minutes.

SUSAN:
For what?

TOM:
Cause that slutty ass of yours is gonna give me some.

SUSAN:
Please not when you're drunk.

TOM:
Who said I was drunk?

SUSAN:
I can smell it all over you.

First Bride

TOM:
Don't you tell me when I'm drunk.

Tom slaps Susan again.

SUSAN:
Okay, I'll be up in five minutes.

TOM:
You swear?

SUSAN:
I swear.

TOM:
Good, cause I would hate to see what happens to you if you if you let me down again.

SUSAN:
When have I ever denied you?

TOM:
When you were off cheating on me is when.

SUSAN:
I give up. Just go upstairs, I'll be up there in five minutes, just like you want.

TOM:
Good.

Tom stumbles up the stairs. He can be heard falling in to walls and flopping on the bed. Susan looks outside again and once again sees Lilith out there. Lilith waves her hand inviting Susan outside.

SUSAN:
I know what I have to do.

Susan grabs a knife and heads upstairs. When she gets up there Tom is passed out on the bed. She walks into the bedroom and the door creaks as she opens it.

TOM:
What the? What is going on?

Susan approaches the bed.

TOM:
Ah, it's you. You finally doing something are ya?

Susan lifts the knife above her head. Tom smacks her ass before noticing the knife raised in the air.

TOM:
What is that? What're you doing? Bringing the dirty dishes up here now?

Susan begins to stab Tom in the chest. Blood splatters all over the bed and the walls. Tom gasps for breath as Susan stabs him. Eventually he gives up and dies.

SUSAN:
See you in hell.

Two children begin crying and Susan drops the knife on the floor. She goes downstairs and outside to where Lilith is waiting.

SUSAN:
I offer my life into your service.

LILITH:
Come, daughter, follow me and I will give you the world.

INT. - BEDROOM – NIGHT

Jeremiah is tossing and turning in his sleep.

DREAM – A SUNSET ON THE BEACH

Jeremiah and HANNA are walking down a beach they are flirting MOS and kissing. Hanna is wearing a blue sundress and Jeremiah is wearing shorts and a t-shirt.

HANNA:
I love you.

JEREMIAH:
I love you too.

Hanna laughs then runs off to a boardwalk that stretches out over the water. Hanna stops under the boardwalk where Jeremiah catches her. They hug and laugh together. Hanna once again runs away, this time on top of the board walk.

JEREMIAH:
Where are you going?

HANNA:
You mean you don't know.

Hanna walks to the end of the board walk with her back turned to Jeremiah. Jeremiah catches up to her and suddenly it is Lilith. Jeremiah looks right into her eyes and red eyes look back at him

JEREMIAH:
Who are you?

LILITH:
You know who I am.

JEREMIAH:
No, I don't

LILITH:
This world will be mine.

JEREMIAH:
I don't know what you're talking about.

LILITH:
You will.

Jeremiah runs to the end of the boardwalk but trips just before he gets there. He looks up and sees Rebecca standing there.

REBECCA:
Beware Lilith, she comes into the world.

JEREMIAH:
What?

First Bride
BACK TO BEDCHAMBER.

     The alarm in the bedchamber goes off. Jeremiah wakes up and groggily turns it off. He sits up in bed and looks confused.

Act 2

INT. - BEDCHAMBER – DAY

Jeremiah is busy getting dressed when the sounds of church bells ringing is heard. He looks up surprised. He grabs his robes and heads out of the room.

INT. - HALLWAY – DAY

As Jeremiah is moving down the hallway he runs into James.

JEREMIAH:
Do you know what's going on?

JAMES:
No idea, I hope it's not another drill.

JEREMIAH:
Why would they run a drill when they know some people will be away?

JAMES:
Does this place ever do things that make sense?

JEREMIAH:
You got a point.

INT. - MEETING ROOM – DAY

Jeremiah and James run into a meeting room where a large crowd of inquisitors have met. Rebecca is off to the side and Jeremiah and James are in the back. Brother Andrews is standing at a raised podium.

BROTHER ANDREWS:
Is everyone here?

Silence.

BROTHER ANDREWS:
Then let us begin. I am glad to say this is not a drill. We have a mission opportunity available if anyone is interested.

IRRITATED INQUISITOR:
What's the mission?

BROTHER ANDREWS:
You will be heading to the north-east corner of the United States to investigate a mass murder.

ARROGANT INQUISITOR:
Isn't that a job for the local police?

BROTHER ANDREWS:
The mass murder happened at an witches coven and we need to determine if something supernatural was involved.

First Bride

IRRITATED INQUISITOR:
This isn't worth my time.

JEREMIAH:
(to James)
You want to go?

JAMES:
(to Jeremiah)
Not really, I'm looking for something with action.

JEREMIAH:
(to James)
That's just like you to.

BROTHER ANDREWS:
Do I have any volunteers?

Jeremiah raises his hand.

JAMES:
(to Jeremiah)
What are you doing?

JEREMIAH:
(to James)
I want to go.

JAMES:
(to Jeremiah)
And leave me here by myself?

JEREMIAH:
(to James)
Then come along.

JAMES:
(to Jeremiah)
No.

BROTHER ANDREWS:
Mr. Carpenter I see you, anyone else?

Rebecca raises her hand.

BROTHER ANDREWS:
Ms. Teabol

ISAAC and JOHN raise their hands.

BROTHER ANDREWS:
Very well, that's all we need. If you four can accompany me. The rest of you are dismissed.

The other inquisitors begin to leave. Jeremiah, Rebecca, Isaac and John stay behind. Brother Andrews opens a door behind the podium.

BROTHER ANDREWS:
This way.

INT. - OFFICE HALLWAY – DAY

The four inquisitors walk through the hallway where other priests are busy behind computers and flipping through books. They follow Brother Andrews to an office at the end of the hall. He opens the door and they all go in.

INT. - OFFICE – DAY

In the office is a desk in front of a window and bookshelves on either side of the room. There are two chairs which Isaac and John sit down in.

BROTHER ANDREWS:
I thank you all for agreeing to go on this mission. I know most others are looking for missions with fighting in them.

ISAAC:
We just like to get out and doing something.

BROTHER ANDREWS:
Believe me, these missions are just as important as the more exciting ones. The young ones just don't seem to realize it.

JOHN:
So what's the deal?

Brother Andrews sits down behind the desk. He pulls out a folder and opens it

BROTHER ANDREWS:
An inquisitor by the name of Allison Redford who works in our New England division in the United States has been keeping a close eye on a coven in her area. She befriended a couple of the witches and when she couldn't get a hold of them she went to investigate and found the entire coven slain.

ISAAC:
Any idea what or who could have done this?

BROTHER ANDREWS:
Allison made it clear that even her friends were very apprehensive about telling her anything so she really doesn't have any information other than what I've given you.

JOHN:
It's kind of vague.

BROTHER ANDERWS:
I realize that, but it's the best I can offer.

JOHN:
When do we leave?

BROTHER ANDREWS:
Tomorrow morning. You'll be taking a private flight out and meeting with Ms. Redford at the airport. Say nothing of this to other inquisitors. Understood?

ISAAC:
No problem.

BROTHER ANDREWS:
Alright, go and get packed and turn in early tonight. It'll be an early morning tomorrow.

JOHN:
Thank you, brother.

EXT. - VATICAN AIRPORT – DAY

    The day is bright and the airport is busy. Planes are busy being taxied around and crowds of people are going in and out of the airport.

INT. - AIRPLANE – DAY

    Jeremiah and Rebecca are seated in their seats and a NERVOUS STEWARDESS is checking everyone's seatbelts.

    HEAD STEWARDESS (V.O.):
Please make sure your tables and chair backs are in the upright and locked position. We will be departing shortly.

    JEREMIAH:
You ever get nervous flying?

    REBECCA:
Not really, I used to when I was younger.

    JEREMIAH:
Do a lot of traveling when you were young?

    REBECCA:
Yeah, until what happened with my sister, my dad wanted us to see all we could see and took us to lots of places. You?

    JEREMIAH:
Besides here, I've never been out of the U.S.

    REBECCA:
Well, that's unfortunate.

    JEREMIAH:
Why do you say that?

    REBECCA:
There's so much to see. I should be asking if you're the one who's going to get nervous.

    JEREMIAH:
(slightly sweating)
I'll be fine.

    REBECCA:
(laughs)
Yeah, okay.

EXT. - RUNWAY – DAY

    The airplane takes off and into the sky.

EXT – U.S. AIRPORT – NIGHT

    ALLISON is waiting by a big white van. She looks impatient as she taps her foot on the ground. After a few seconds, Jeremiah, Rebecca, Isaac and John are seen coming out of the terminal. Allison waves her hand to get their attention.

    ALLISON:
John, Isaac, over here.

    JOHN:
There's Allison there.

JEREMIAH:
How do you know her?

JOHN:
My first mission was with Allison.

JEREMIAH:
How'd that go?

JOHN:
Not as expected.

ISAAC:
(laughs)
Nothing ever does.

JEREMIAH:
Have you known her a long time?

JOHN:
About five years.

JEREMIAH:
How long have you and Allison been inquisitors?

JOHN:
Me, five years. Allison, close to ten.

JEREMIAH:
That's a long time in this line of work.

ISAAC:
That's why if she tells you to do something, you best do it.

JEREMIAH:
Why's that?

JOHN:
Cause nine times out of ten, she's right.

> *They meet up with Allison at the van.*

JOHN:
Allison, good to see you again.

ALLISON:
John, likewise.
(points at Jeremiah and Rebecca)
Who are these two?

JOHN:
Jeremiah and Rebecca, a couple of recent recruits.

ALLISON:
I don't need recent recruits here, I need experienced people.

JOHN:
That bad?

ALLISON:
Yes.

First Bride

JOHN:
Well we can't send them back.

REBECCA:
I have no intention of heading back now.

ALLISON:
Fine but you do as I tell you, you got that?

REBECCA:
Got it.

ALLISON:
Alright, get in the van.

They all get into the van and the van drives off.

INT. - VAN – NIGHT

JEREMIAH:
So where are we heading first?

ALLISON:
We're going to go to my place and crash there for the night, then we'll head to the temple tomorrow.

JEREMIAH:
Why leave it till tomorrow?

ALLISON:
A little gung-ho here aren't we?

JEREMIAH:
Not at all.

ALLISON:
Yeah okay.

JEREMIAH:
I'm serious.

ALLISON:
I would just rather have you all rested and ready to go rather than sleepy and dragging your asses the whole time.

JEREMIAH:
The longer we leave it the more likely the cops will find it though don't you think?

ALLISON:
That's true, but the temple is so secluded it could take them a long time to even know it's there.

REBECCA:
Wouldn't friends or family members of the members wonder what's going on?

ALLISON:
Most of the members are single.

REBECCA:
How do you know that?

ALLISON:
I had friends inside that told me.

JEREMIAH:
What about the unsingle ones.

ALLISON:
Their families were used to them being gone days at a time.

JEREMIAH:
So how do you know so much about the people but very little about the coven itself.

ALLISON:
Excuse me?

JEREMIAH:
Sorry, but Brother Andrews told us you didn't know that much about them.

ALLISON:
That's partially true. I don't know specific names or rituals of the group but I know the coven was a decent size and composed of all women.

ISAAC:
Why all women?

ALLISON:
My friends hinted at the fact that most of these women came from abusive or controlling homes. Those that were had left their husbands and rallied together. I told a great sob story about an imaginary ex-husband of my own. That's why the two girls I was friends with trusted me.

ISAAC:
Ah, I see.

EXT. - ALLISON'S HOUSE – NIGHT

The van pulls into a small driveway that leads to a medium sized white bungalow. The house looks a little old and shabby but good nonetheless. The five of them get casually out of the van and stretch.

JOHN:
This is the hole they've got you shacked up in?

ALLISON:
You know that the Inquisition pays for your housing, but that it's not always the best in the world.

JOHN:
I know but still. They could've done better than this.

ALLISON:
This is actually quite typical. Not a lot of rich folks around here. If they gave me a top-of-the-line home it would really stand out.

JOHN:
True.

ALLISON:
Come on in, I'll show you around.

INT. - HOUSE – NIGHT

The front door opens and the five inquisitors enter. They walk right into a kitchen. There is a living room to the right and a back hallway that leads to two bedrooms. There is a set of stairs going down beside the front door.

First Bride
ALLISON:
Rebecca, you'll be staying in the bedroom down the hallway to the right. The left is my room don't go in there.

REBECCA:
Okay.

ALLISON:
Boys you'll be staying in the basement.

The boys head downstairs and find a completely open room with four bunk beds along the walls.

JEREMIAH:
I see we're living in luxury.

JOHN:
Get used to it, this actually isn't that bad.

JEREMIAH:
Seriously?

JOHN:
Seriously.

EXT. - STREET WITH HOTEL – NIGHT

Lilith walks up to the front of a hotel. Susan is with her along with three other women. Lilith turns towards the hotel.

SUSAN:
Mistress, what's going on?

LILITH:
We await another sister.

A light turns on in a second floor room. Screaming is heard and blood shoots across one of the windows. A few seconds later a woman walks out of the front of the hotel and stands in front of Lilith.

MUDEROUS WOMAN:
Mistress, I offer my life into your service.

LILITH:
I accept your life into my service.

EXT. - TEMPLE – DAY

The white van carrying Allison, Jeremiah, Rebecca, John and Isaac pulls into the parking lot of the temple. The parking lot has thirty cars in it. The five inquisitors get out of the van.

JOHN:
Looks like we missed quite the party.

ALLISON:
Trust me, it's a party you'd be glad you missed.

JOHN:
True.

The five of them walk up to the front door.

INT. - TEMPLE FOYER – DAY

The foyer door opens up and the five of them walk inside. Rebecca gags and covers her mouth.

REBECCA:
That smell is horrible.

ALLISON:
It's the smell of death.

REBECCA:
It's awful.

ALLISON:
If you can't handle it, you're in the wrong line of work.

REBECCA:
I'm sure I'll get used to it.

ALLISON:
Better hope so.
(pause)
Jeremiah and Rebecca, you take the office. John, Isaac and I will investigate the sanctuary.

JEREMIAH:
No problem, anything specific we're looking for?

ALLISON:
Any hint at what happened here.

JEREMIAH:
Got it.

Jeremiah and Rebecca open the door into the office.

INT. - OFFICE – DAY

Jeremiah and Rebecca enter into the office and look around.

JEREMIAH:
Cozy place.

REBECCA:
They got quite the library here.

JEREMIAH:
Any idea what books we should take?

REBECCA:
No clue, you think they'd be mad if we took all of them?

JEREMIAH:
Probably, but if we missed something they wouldn't let us live it down.

REBECCA:
I agree.

JEREMIAH:
I'll go pull the van up to the front door.

REBECCA:
Okay.

Jeremiah leaves the office. Rebecca sits down behind the desk and opens up the lower right hand drawer. Inside is a bunch of file folders all listed with names. She flips through the names and gasps then pulls out a file folder.

INSERT – FILE FOLDER

The file has the name Redford, Allison on it.

BACK TO OFFICE

REBECCA:
Allison, what were they going to do?

INSERT – FILE FOLDER

Rebecca opens up the file folder and there is a post-it note that says "to exterminate" in red ink. Rebecca gasps.

BACK TO OFFICE

Rebecca gets up and heads out of the office.

INT. - FOYER – DAY

REBECCA:
(yelling)
Allison.

ALLISON (V.O.):
What?

Jeremiah shows up behind Rebecca.

JEREMIAH:
What's going on?

REBECCA:
Look at this.

Rebecca opens up the file.

JEREMIAH:
You go talk to her, I'll start loading the books.

ALLISON:
Rebecca? What do you want?

Rebecca walks up to Allison and shows her the file.

REBECCA:
Looks like you got lucky.

ALLISON:
They must have known I was trying to infiltrate them.

REBECCA:
Or they must have seen you as a threat.

ALLISON:
Could be. Or I was just being too nosy.
(pause)
What are you two doing?

REBECCA:
We're loading the library into the van, just so we don't miss anything.

ALLISON:
Good idea. Come in here and start copying some of the symbols down in here.

REBECCA:
Okay.

Rebecca follows Allison into the chapel.

INT. - CHAPEL – DAY

Rebecca covers her mouth in shock when she sees the gory mess laying in the middle of the room.
John is kneeling down along the edge of the bodies taking samples and making notes.

JOHN:
It doesn't look like a weapon was used.

ALLISON:
What do you mean?

JOHN:
A gun would leave gunshot wounds and knives would leave clean cuts. These puncture wounds look
like they were ripped or torn.

ALLISON:
You saying someone did this with their bare hands?

JOHN:
That's exactly what it looks like.

Rebecca takes a pad of paper and starts copying down symbols.

ISAAC:
So how do we clean this all up?

ALLISON:
We'll burn the place down.
        (pause, then yells)
Jeremiah.

JEREMIAH (V.O.):
Yeah?

ALLISON:
You done with those books.

JEREMAIH:
Yeah.

ALLISON:
Alright, lets get out of here.

The inquisitors gather up their notes and gear and head out of the room

EXT. - TEMPLE – DAY

ALLISON:
Get the gas.

First Bride
    ISAAC:
Done.

    Isaac goes into the back of the van and takes a gas container out and heads back into the temple. John grabs a second container and heads in as well.

    ALLISON:
We need to get out of here.

    JEREMIAH:
Why's that?

    ALLISON:
I have a feeling the cops are on their way.

    John and Isaac emerge from the temple. Everyone except John get into the van. The van pulls away. John lights a match then throws it into the temple. The temple erupts in flames. John gets in the van and they drive off.

INT. - VAN – DAY

    As they drive down the road a cop cruiser drives by them.

    REBECCA:
Looks like we got out of there just in time.

    ALLISON:
I knew it.

    JOHN:
Let's get out of here before they come after us.

EXT. - TEMPLE – DAY

    Constable JOHNSON steps out of the cruiser and looks at the temple.

    JOHNSON:
Holy shit.
    (into his radio)
We need the fire department at that church on the third line.

    DISPATCHER (V.O.):
Ten-four.

    JOHNSON:
Who would've done this?

INT. - ALLISON'S HOUSE LIVING ROOM – NIGHT

INSERT – T.V. SCREEN

    The local news is playing on the T.V. A female SERIOUS ANCHOR is sitting behind a desk in a business suit. A banner with "POLICE WARNING" in the upper right hand corner is seen.

    SERIOUS ANCHOR:
Police have issued a warning tonight about a group of women making their way through the countryside. Although unwilling to give details of the situation they say that the women are dangerous and responsible for a series of murders in our area.

    A sketch of Lilith appears in the upper right hand corner.

SERIOUS ANCHOR:
This is a sketch of the woman thought to be their ring-leader. If you spot the women, police warn to stay away and call nine-one-one immediately.

BACK TO LIVING ROOM

Jeremiah, Allison and Isaac are sitting on a couch watching the news.

JEREMIAH:
Sounds serious.

ISAAC:
You think it's related to our case?

ALLISON:
Might be, but I'm not jumping to any conclusions.

ISAAC:
Smart.

ALLISON:
(laughs)
That's why I'm the boss.
(pause)
So what's with all these books you two brought here?

Allison moves to the kitchen.

INT. - KITCHEN – NIGHT

Rebecca is sitting at a table with John flipping through a book. The sketch of the symbols in the sanctuary is on the table. Jeremiah and Isaac come in and sit down and grab a book.

JEREMIAH:
Thought they might help. Any luck?

REBECCA:
No, not yet.

JOHN:
If you hadn't emptied out an entire library we might be having more luck.

JEREMIAH:
Knowing my luck, if we left books behind they would be the ones that we needed.

ISAAC:
I tend to agree with Jeremiah.

JOHN:
Fine then.

Jeremiah flips a page. He stares intently at the page then looks at the sketch.

INSERT – BOOK PAGE

Jeremiah lifts the sketch up to the book. The sketch and symbol on the page match.

BACK TO KITCHEN

JEREMIAH:
I think I found something.

First Bride

JOHN:
What're you talking about?

JEREMIAH:
I got a match for this symbol.

JOHN:
I've been sitting here for hours going through these books and you get it with one shot.

JEREMIAH:
Someone is smiling down on me.

ALLISON:
Oh don't start.

Jeremiah laughs.

JOHN:
Well don't keep us waiting. What does it say?

JEREMIAH:
(with a look of shock)
Apparently the coven was a group that worships Lilith.

REBECCA:
Who is that?

ALLISON:
I don't know, I've never heard of her.

JEREMIAH:
It says here that groups that worship her are always composed of mostly women. They are usually associated with another group of all men that worship a demon named Samael.

JOHN:
Any idea who that is?

ALLISON:
Again, no.

ISAAC:
Well this isn't helping.

ALLISON:
Does it say anything else?

JEREMIAH:
Yeah it says that they perform long rituals that can take years to complete.

REBECCA:
To do what?

JEREMIAH:
Summon her.

REBECCA:
What's with the look of shock?

JEREMIAH:
Oh, it's nothing.

ALLISON:
Spill it, what's wrong?

JEREMIAH:
Before we got recruited for this mission I had a dream that had Lilith in it.

JOHN:
Really? What happened?

JEREMIAH:
At first she was my ex, and then she transformed into this Lilith and chased me.

REBECCA:
Did you get away?

JEREMIAH:
It was hard, I was about to be caught when you...
    (points at Rebecca)
...saved me.

REBECCA:
What do I have to do with this?

JEREMIAH:
I don't know.

ALLISON:
Well I would rule it out as coincidence, but this is just too much of one to write it off.

JOHN:
So what do we do?

ALLISON:
I'll email Brother Andrews and see if he has any information that can be of use.

    Allison leaves into the living room. The group is silent for a few seconds.

JOHN:
So anything else you hiding from us?

JEREMIAH:
No, that's it.

ISAAC:
Did that picture they showed on the news look like the same woman?

JEREMIAH:
Quite a bit yeah.

JOHN:
You didn't put two and two together at that point.

JEREMIAH:
No, I didn't.

REBECCA:
Hey take it easy on him.

JOHN:
This is just weird.

First Bride
   REBECCA:
Why do you say that?

   JOHN:
Cause, I don't really believe in that stuff.

   JEREMIAH:
But I didn't say it was anything.

   JOHN:
Still, it's a little freaky.

   Allison re-enters the room.

   ALLISON:
So I sent the email off. Hopefully we'll hear something soon.

Act 3

INT. - ALLISON'S HOUSE – DAY

A knocking is heard at the front door. Allison rushes up to answer it.

ALLISON:
Who could this be?

Allison opens the door. Brother Andrews is standing on the other side.

ALLISON:
(surprised)
Brother, what are you doing here?

BROTHER ANDREWS:
I've come concerning your email.

ALLISON:
What about it?

BROTHER ANDREWS:
May I come inside?

ALLISON:
Yes, of course.

Brother Andrews comes into the house. Jeremiah, Rebecca, John and Isaac are all sitting at the dinner table eating breakfast.

JOHN:
Brother Andrews, what are you doing here?

BROTHER ANDREWS:
I needed to talk to all of you.

ISAAC:
But aren't you supposed to be in the Vatican?

BROTHER ANDREWS:
I've been monitoring you from the local parish.

JOHN:
Creepy.

BROTHER ANDREWS:
I'm sorry, but with new recruits it is required.

JOHN:
Still.

ALLISON:
So what was so important about that email that you had to come here.

BROTHER ANDREWS:
The coven that was murdered, is it true they worshiped Lilith?

ALLISON:
From all we could gather, yeah.

BROTHER ANDREWS:
We must act fast.

ALLISON:
Why's that?

BROTHER ANDREWS:
If we don't, we are all in grave trouble.

ALLISON:
Again, why?

BROTHER ANDREWS:
If she's doing what she did the last time...

JEREMIAH:
Last time? There was a last time?

BROTHER ANDREWS:
Yes, there was.

ALLISON:
And why haven't I heard of this?

BROTHER ANDREWS:
It was kept confidential.

ALLISON:
I got a feeling this isn't going to go well.

BROTHER ANDREWS:
If we don't act fast, then no it won't.

ALLISON:
What's she intending?

BROTHER ANDREWS:
Like I said, if it's a repeat of last time, she will recruit a group of women and make them her guardians. She will then meet up with a demon named Samael to raise an army.

JOHN:
Raise an army how?

BROTHER ANDREWS:
By giving birth to one.

JOHN:
Say what?

BROTHER ANDREWS:
I'm sorry, you probably don't know the whole story.

ALLISON:
Please, enlighten us.

BROTHER ANDREWS:
Almost everyone knows the story about Adam and Eve. What most people don't know is that Eve was actually Adam's second wife.

ALLISON:
You're kidding me.

BROTHER ANDREWS:
I'm afraid not.

JOHN:
Go on.

BROTHER ANDREWS:
In the book of Genesis, chapter one tells of man and woman being created on the sixth day.

ISAAC:
Yeah, that's common knowledge.

BROTHER ANDREWS:
There is a second account of women being created in chapter two.

ALLISON:
Haven't scholars always said it was just a deeper explanation of the creation story?

BROTHER ANDREWS:
That's what we thought for centuries, but we were wrong.

JEREMIAH:
Okay, so how'd Eve end up needing to be created?

BROTHER ANDREWS:
Although it's not in the Bible, other texts reveal the story to us. Lilith refused to take on co-rulership of the Earth.

REBECCA:
She wanted it all for herself.

BROTHER ANDREWS:
That, or she saw it as submissive and wouldn't stand for it.

ALLISON:
So then what?

BROTHER ANDREWS:
Lilith then called on the ineffible name and was taken out of Eden.

JOHN:
Whose name did she speak?

BROTHER ANDREWS:
We don't know for certain, but we're assuming it was Lucifer's.

JOHN:
Great, now we're dealing with the devil.

BROTHER ANDREWS:
Kind of.

ALLISON:
Go on.

First Bride

BROTHER ANDREWS:
While she was being taken away, the angel Gabriel pleaded with her to go back to Adam but she refused. She was then placed down on the bank of the Euphrates where she met Samael and bore his demonic children.

REBECCA:
So what you're saying...

BROTHER ANDREWS:
If we don't stop Lilith, she'll meet up with Samael and give birth to an army that will be difficult to stop.

ALLISON:
Did they stop her in time last time?

BROTHER ANDREWS:
Barely, but yes. We lost a lot of good inquisitors then.

JOHN:
So how are we five supposed to stop...how many of them?

BROTHER ANDREWS:
Lilith plus thirteen women and whatever children she manages to bear.

JEREMIAH:
I knew I should have stayed in bed this morning.

ALLISON:
How do we get rid of Lilith?

BROTHER ANDREWS:
Just killing her won't do, you'll have to exorcise her.

ALLISON:
Will a typical exorcism work?

BROTHER ANDREWS:
No, but this should.

Brother Andrews hands Allison a piece of paper. Allison quickly reads it over.

ALLISON:
This seems simple enough.

BROTHER ANDREWS:
It always seems simple in theory.

ALLISON:
That's true.

JOHN:
So any idea where Lilith is heading to?

BROTHER ANDREWS:
We have another inquisitor south of here watching a coven of Samael worshipers. I've made contact with him and am in the process of mobilizing as many local inquisitors as I can.
(hands Allison a piece of paper)
Here is the number you can get a hold of him at.

Allison takes and looks at the piece of paper.

ALLISON:
Joshua? Isn't he a little introverted?

BROTHER ANDREWS:
Yes, he's a little difficult to work with but he's been very successful so far. He'll have more information that will be useful to you. But I must be going.

ALLISON:
Thank you brother.

BROTHER ANDREWS:
You're welcome. For what it's worth, good luck.

ALLISON:
Thanks.

Brother Andrews leaves. Allison closes the door and sighs.

EXT. - DARK STREET – NIGHT

JOSHUA is waiting in the shadow of a building watching a PARANOID MAN as he walks down the street. The man seems to be trying to make sure no one is following him but he fails to notice Joshua. Joshua curses when his cellphone rings.

JOSHUA:
Dammit.

The paranoid man looks at Joshua then runs off. Joshua answers his cellphone.

JOSHUA:
Hello?

ALLISON (V.O.):
Joshua, it's Allison.

JOSHUA:
Took you a little while to call.

ALLISON: (V.O.):
Yeah, we were trying to plan out our next move.

JOSHUA (V.O.):
And what do you got?

ALLISON:
Well we'll try to intercept Lilith but we want a back up plan in case that doesn't work.

JOSHUA (V.O.):
Good idea.

ALLISON:
Any idea where Lilith plans on meeting Samael?

JOSHUA:
There's an old warehouse that they tend to meet in. It's fairly secluded. So if they're planning what we think they're planning it will probably be there.

ALLISON:
Alright, try to make any inquisitors that Brother Andrews can muster comfortable. Once we have any news, we'll let you know.

JOSHUA (V.O.):
Why do I have to do it?

First Bride
>ALLISON:
Please?

>JOSHUA:
Fine.

>*Joshua hangs up his cellphone and tries to regain his bearings. The man he was following suddenly jumps from behind him. Joshua hits the man in the head as the man leaps.*

>JOSHUA:
You don't want to do this.

>PARANOID MAN:
What do you want?

>JOSHUA:
When is Samael being summoned?

>PARANOID MAN:
(snarls)
I don't know what you're talking about.

>JOSHUA:
Don't bullshit me, I know who you are.

>*Paranoid Man tries to kick at Joshua's feet. Joshua jumps out of the way and kicks the man in the head. The man rolls off down a dark alley.*

>PARANOID MAN:
Just leave us alone.

>JOSHUA:
Can't do that.

>PARANOID MAN:
You can't stop us.

>JOSHUA:
We can try.

>PARANOID MAN:
Who? You and your precious Inquisition?

>JOSHUA:
You'd be surprised what we can do.

>PARANOID MAN:
Just stay away from us.

>*Paranoid Man gets up and runs down the alley. Joshua tries to keep up but quickly falls behind. The Paranoid Man turns a corner. Joshua turns the corner and runs into a busy crowd. Paranoid Man is gone.*

>JOSHUA:
Shit. Allison you owe me big time.

INT. - HANNA'S HOUSE – NIGHT

>*HANNA is busy packing a bag and her WORRIED MOM is in the room with her.*

>WORRIED MOM:
But Hanna, why do you have to do this?

HANNA:
I don't know I just feel like I have to.

WORRIED MOM:
Are you sure this is wise?

HANNA:
What are you talking about?

WORRIED MOM:
Well ever since that incident at the museum you've suffering from depression.

HANNA:
Don't start with me again.

WORRIED MOM:
But it's affected you so much.

HANNA:
Mom, I'm fine really.

WORRIED MOM:
Hanna, honey, this could just be worrying.

HANNA:
Worrying over what?

WORRIED MOM:
You feel guilty for leaving Jeremiah.

HANNA:
That has nothing to do with this.

WORRIED MOM:
I wish I could believe you.

HANNA:
Sure I left him, and it was a mistake, but I'm over that now.

WORRIED MOM:
Is that why you still cry yourself to sleep?

Hanna sighs.

WORRIED MOM:
Yes I know about that.

HANNA:
Yeah there's nights I wish he was here.

WORRIED MOM:
I'm sure you can just call him and everything will be fine again.

HANNA:
No, this has nothing to do with him, I already told you that.

WORRIED MOM:
I don't believe that.

HANNA:
Well you should.

First Bride

WORRIED MOM:
Then what is this about?

HANNA:
I don't know, I just have this feeling that I have to leave for awhile.

WORRIED MOM:
Then I'm worried about your safety.

HANNA:
I'm not going to hurt myself.

WORRIED MOM:
You have before.

HANNA:
I'm over that.

WORRIED MOM:
Again I wish I could believe you.

HANNA:
You can't stop me from going.

WORRIED MOM:
No, you're right I can't.

Hanna closes her suitcase.

HANNA:
Then please leave me alone.

WORRIED MOM:
I can't do that either.

HANNA:
Well you're going to have to, because I'm ready to go, so I'm leaving.

WORRIED MOM:
Okay, but when you come home can you please consider moving back home?

HANNA:
Not that again.

WORRIED MOM:
Your father would love to have you back at home.

HANNA:
I thought he didn't want to talk to me.

WORRIED MOM:
That was just anger talking. Every now and then he talks about how much he misses you.

HANNA:
I'll consider it.

WORRIED MOM:
Are you serious this time?

HANNA:
Yes.

WORRIED MOM:
You've said that before.

HANNA:
I mean it this time.

WORRIED MOM:
Alright, just be safe out there okay?

HANNA:
Yes mom.

WORRIED MOM:
Alright, goodbye honey.

Hanna and Worried Mom hug.

HANNA:
Bye, mom.

EXT. - RAINY STREET – NIGHT

Police are barricading a rainy street that on one end opens up to stores and mountains. The police are barricading a bridge. They are all armed with shotguns and service revolvers and waiting behind their cruisers.

ARROGANT COP:
So, Johnson, done banging your partner?

JOHNSON:
We're not doing that anymore.

ARROGANT COP:
Did your wife catch you?

JOHNSON:
You could say that.

ARROGANT COP:
And she stayed with you?

JOHNSON:
Let's just say we're working things out.

ARROGANT COP:
That doesn't sound good.

JOHNSON:
No, it's not.

ARROGANT COP:
I don't let my wife catch me with my women.

JOHNSON:
One day she will.

ARROGANT COP:
Nah, she won't.

JOHNSON:
Don't be so sure.

First Bride

ARROGANT COP:
It won't happen.

JOHNSON:
Yeah, okay.

ARROGANT COP:
So what happened at that church in the country?

JOHNSON:
Like I reported, it was burned to the ground.

ARROGANT COP:
Weren't there a bunch of bodies in there?

JOHNSON:
Yeah.

ARROGANT COP:
Fun.

JOHNSON:
Luckily we could track down the people we think were responsible.

ARROGANT COP:
A bunch of angry, man hating broads, this should be fun.

JOHNSON:
Makes you wish you called in sick.

ARROGANT COP:
I can deal with them.

Lilith and twelve women come from around a corner.

ARROGANT COP:
Speaking of the devil.

The rain starts to fall harder.

JOHNSON:
(looking up to the sky)
You believe in bad omens?

ARROGANT COP:
Nope, why do you?

JOHNSON:
I never used to.

ARROGANT COP:
(raises shotgun)
Relax, this'll be over before dinner.

JOHNSON:
Let's hope you're right.

ARROGANT COP:
(to Lilith)
Stop where you are, you are all under arrest.

Lilith and the women start walking towards them.

ARROGANT COP:
Brave, bitches.

JOHNSON:
Just be careful.

ARROGANT COP:
Always am.

Arrogant cop fires a shot off into the air. The women keep closing. They have a look of determination in their eyes.

ARROGANT COP:
I said freeze.

The women stops and Lilith steps forward.

LILITH:
We stop for no man.

Lilith raises her hands and pushes them forward. The cop cruisers push backward crushing four of the cops between them. The cops try to push the cars to free themselves.

ARROGANT COP:
Holy shit. Open fire.

The four unpinned cops start opening fire. Lilith raises her hands again and all the bullets avoid the group. The ladies then run forward and attack the police.

ARROGANT COP:
Dammit, I gotta reload.

JOHNSON:
Same here.
(points at the other two cops)
You two, hold them off.

The women reach the four pinned cops and begin ripping them apart. The two cops with Johnson and the Arrogant Cop open fire and manage to drop two of the women. Susan and Lilith crawl over the cruisers and lunge at the two firing cops.

ARROGANT COP:
Shit, we gotta fall back.

JOHNSON:
To where?

ARROGANT COP:
There I'm reloaded.

Lilith rips the throat out of one cop and Susan pulls her fingers out of the other cops eyes. Lilith and Susan turn towards Johnson and the Arrogant cop as the other eleven women get over the cars.

LILITH:
Your end is here.

ARROGANT COP:
Just try it.

Arrogant Cop tries to fire his shotgun but it jams.

First Bride
ARROGANT COP:
Oh shit.

Lilith and the women charge at Johnson and Arrogant Cop. As they swarm over them blood seeps from between the women and they can be heard screaming.

EXT. - ALLISON'S HOUSE – DAY

The five Inquisitors are outside loading up the van. Allison is standing outside the van scrolling through her phone.

JOHN:
So where are we heading?

ALLISON:
We're going to try and track Lilith down.

JOHN:
And what if we can't?

ALLISON:
Then we'll rendezvous with Joshua and wait for Lilith to show up.

ISAAC:
Can I mention I think this is a bad plan?

ALLISON:
No, but why do you say that?

ISAAC:
If we don't track her down we're going to have to face one pissed off woman along with her demon lover. The odds aren't good for us.

ALLISON:
Then what would you suggest?

Silence.

ALLISON:
That's what I thought.

JOHN:
The countryside around here is pretty massive, what makes you think we can find her?

ALLISON:
We may get lucky.

JOHN:
That's a pretty big may.

ALLISON:
Again, what would you suggest?

JOHN:
I don't know.

ALLISON:
Well we're not going to be effective just sitting here waiting for something to happen.

Jeremiah comes out of the house.

JEREMIAH:
Allison, you should see this.

ALLISON:
What is it?

JEREMIAH:
The news.

INT. - ALLISON'S HOUSE – DAY

Allison walks into the house behind Jeremiah and into the living room.

INSERT – T.V.

The Serious Anchor is on screen.

SERIOUS ANCHOR:
This just in. Police barricaded a roadway late last night in an attempt to apprehend the women they believe responsible for the series of murders.

The news shows a scene of emergency teams at the rainy street. AMBITIOUS REPORTER is standing there with SHERIFF ADAMS.

AMBITIOUS REPORTER:
We're here at the state line where cops have been brutally killed at the hands of a series of women they believe responsible for the murder of husbands and boyfriends. I have Sheriff Adams here to comment. Sheriff what happened?

SHERIFF ADAMS:
We underestimated the deadliness of the women and are now pulling back to consider our options.

AMBITIOUS REPORTER:
Have they crossed the state border?

SHERIFF ADAMS:
Yes we believe they have.

AMBITIOUS REPORTER:
Are the citizens of this state safe or is there still need to worry?

SHERIFF ADAMS:
I would still be careful and if you suspect anything to not hesitate to give us a call.

AMBITIOUS REPORTER:
What about the other state's police? Have you forewarned them?

SHERIFF ADAMS:
Yes we have forewarned them, but they have been unable to track them down. The mountainous terrain makes it difficult.

AMBITIOUS REPORTER:
Thank you Sheriff.

BACK TO LIVING ROOM.

JEREMIAH:
What do you think?

ALLISON:
We know where to start looking at least.

First Bride
JEREMIAH:
What about the deaths?

ALLISON:
We're better trained than cops, but we still need to be careful.

JOHN:
I think this is a little to convenient.

ALLISON:
We'll take what we can get.

JOHN:
I don't like the look of this at all.

ALLISON:
We don't really have much of a choice at this point.

JOHN:
Still.

EXT. - ALLISON'S HOUSE – DAY

Allison, Jeremiah and John come out of the house.

ALLISON:
Everyone ready to go?

ISAAC:
As ready as we're gonna be.

ALLISON:
Alright, let's go.

EXT. - BUSY PARKING LOT – DAY

Hanna parks her car and gets out. She looks around and walks out of the parking lot.

EXT. - BUSY STREET CORNER – DAY

Hanna walks out to the corner where traffic is driving by and crowds of people are walking by. There is a bench on the inside side of the corner. Hanna looks at it and gets up on the bench.

HANNA:
(loudly)
Beware, the dark lady comes.

People nearby look at her strangely and pick up their step to get away from her.

HANNA:
The end has come and all man will pay for their crimes.

ANGRY MAN:
Shut up lady.

HANNA:
The day is coming when this world will burn before her rule.

ANGRY MAN:
I'll burn you if you don't shut up.

A police cruiser pulls up and NEW RECRUIT and OLD COP get out.

HANNA:
Repent man, and she may spare you.

NEW RECRUIT:
Alright lady, let's get moving.

HANNA:
No.

New Recruit starts to pull Hanna down.

HANNA:
No, you will pay for your sin.

NEW RECRUIT:
I'm sure.

Hanna starts to fight but New Recruit handcuffs her and pulls her into the back of the cruiser.

INT. - POLICE CAR – DAY

HANNA:
No, I must spread the word for all to hear.

OLD COP:
You'll be able to spread the word all you want where you're going.

HANNA:
You will burn. You will burn with the rest of man.

OLD COP:
Listen lady, I'm a week away from retirement. I don't need this right now.

HANNA:
You will never see that day, I promise you.

INT. - JOSHUA'S HOUSE – DAY

A doorbell rings and Joshua walks up and opens the door. A SUSPICIOUS MAN in casual clothes and a traveling bag is standing there.

JOSHUA:
Can I help you?

SUSPICIOUS MAN:
Yeah, I gotta call and apparently we're meeting here for a mission?

JOSHUA:
Yeah, we are. What parish you from?

SUSPICIOUS MAN:
I'm from Boston.

JOSHUA:
That's a bit of a ways away.

SUSPICIOUS MAN:
Yeah, but I can't refuse a call. Are you gonna invite me in?

JOSHUA:
Alright, fine come in. There are bunks in the basement some people have already arrive, make yourself comfortable.

First Bride
SUSPICIOUS MAN:
Excellent, thank you.

The Suspicious Man heads down a set of stairs near the back of the house and goes down.

INT. - JOSHUA'S BASMENT – DAY

The basement is laid out with a hallway and two rooms on each side of the hall. There are two men, EAGER INQUISITOR and NERVOUS INQUISITOR here talking to each other.

NERVOUS INQUISITOR:
So what do you think is going to happen?

EAGER INQUISITOR:
Well I imagine once we get the call we'll head out and engage this Samael demon.

NERVOUS INQUISITOR:
I've never fought something like this before, I'm nervous.

EAGER INQUISITOR:
It shouldn't be a problem, as long as you know your exorcisms.

NERVOUS INQUISITOR:
I'm pretty sure I remember them all.

SUSPICIOUS MAN:
Hey there, how are we today?

EAGER INQUISITOR:
Good, yourself?

SUSPICIOUS MAN:
Pretty good, thanks. Is it okay if I take this room?
(points at first bedroom)

EAGER INQUISITOR:
Yeah go ahead.

SUSPICIOUS MAN:
Excellent.

INT. - FIRST BEDROOM – DAY

The Suspicious Man walks into the bedroom and puts his bag down. He opens it up and pulls out an AK-47. He then walks out of the room.

INT. - JOSHUA'S BASEMENT – DAY

SUSPICIOUS MAN:
Hey.

NERVOUS INQUISITOR:
What?

Suspicious Man fires the AK-47 and hits the Nervous Inquisitor right in the head. Blood and brains splatter on the wall behind him and he slumps to the floor, dead.

EAGER INQUISITOR:
Holy shit.

SUSPICIOUS MAN:
Time for you to die.

Suspicious Man shoots at Eager Inquisitor, but misses. Eager Inquisitor lunges at him and manages to grapple with the gun. The two wrestle for control of the gun and Suspicious Man manages to throw Eager Inquisitor off.

SUSPICIOUS MAN:
Die infidel.

Suspicious Man shoots Eager Inquisitor in the chest. Blood soaks the carpet and the inquisitor gasps for a few breaths before dying. Suspicious man turns around and sees Joshua at the top of the stairs with a handgun.

JOSHUA:
You were saying.

SUSPICIOUS MAN:
You can't stop us.

JOSHUA:
We can try.

Joshua shoots Suspicious Man in the head, he falls and dies.

EXT. - REST STOP – DAY

The inquisitors van pulls up to a rest stop and Allison gets out of the van. She spreads a map across the hood of the van and the rest of the inquisitors get out.

JOHN:
Were we able to get back on track?

ALLISON:
I think so.

JOHN:
That town was pretty blocked up, too bad we couldn't get through there.

ALLISON:
With what happened last night, I'm not surprised.

JOHN:
This is the same road then?

ALLISON:
Yeah, according to the map anyway.

JOHN:
Alright, I'm going to start asking questions of the people working here. Hopefully one of them have seen something.

ALLISON:
Yeah go ahead.

Allison starts looking around. She stops and stares intently at something.

ALLISON:
What the?

Allison goes into the van, grabs a pair of binoculars and looks into the mountainside.

ALLISON:
(yelling)
Jeremiah.

First Bride
    JEREMIAH:
Yeah?

    ALLISON:
Come here.

      Jeremiah comes running up.

    JEREMIAH:
What's up?

    ALLISON:
Take these ...
      (gives Jeremiah the binoculars)
... do they look familiar?

    JEREMIAH:
Huh?

      Jeremiah looks into the mountainside.

INSERT – VIEW FROM BINOCULARS

      Lilith and the ten remaining women move across the view.

BACK TO REST STOP

    JEREMIAH:
Yeah, the one woman does.

    ALLISON:
Who does it look like?

    JEREMIAH:
It looks like the Lilith from my dream.

    ALLISON:
Seriously?

    JEREMIAH:
Yeah.

    ALLISON:
Shit.

    JEREMIAH:
This could just be coincidence.

    ALLISON:
I don't think so.
      (yelling)
Everyone, over here now.

      The others come running.

    ISAAC:
What's up?

    ALLISON:
We've found them.

JOHN:
What? Are you serious?

ALLISON:
Yes, Jeremiah identified her as the woman from his dream.

JOHN:
Sorry, if I'm a little skeptical.

JEREMIAH:
I swear she looks the exact same.

ISAAC:
What do you want to do?

ALLISON:
I can't take the risk that it isn't her.

ISAAC:
I agree.

ALLISON:
Everyone, get your gear together, we're going up the mountain and going after her.

JOHN:
Yes, ma'am.

EXT. - MOUTAINSIDE – DAY

Lilith and the ten women are walking through the forests. A roadway is in front of them. Lilith and women keep walking. A look of anger crosses her face as the van suddenly pulls up on the road.

LILITH:
Stop my sisters, we have a job to do.

SUSAN:
Are they trying to stop us?

LILITH:
They will not succeed.

SUSAN:
I agree, mistress.

The women stretch out. The five inquisitors all get out Allison is carrying an MP5, Isaac is carrying an AK-47, John is carrying an M-7, Jeremiah is carrying a shotgun and Rebecca is carrying a handgun.

ALLISON:
Everyone, keep your weapons trained on Lilith, we take her down the others should scatter.

JOHN:
Don't be afraid to defend yourself however if they come after you.

The women start to emerge from the forest. Allison takes a shot at Lilith but it goes wide.

LILITH:
Kill them.

The women rush at the inquisitors. John fires his gun at a woman and fills her with bullet holes. The woman drops twitching.

First Bride
JOHN:
That's right, stay down.

Isaac begins firing his AK at another woman. The woman dives to the side and the shots all miss.

ISAAC:
Damn she was fast.

ALLISON:
Keep focused, we're outnumbered they can easily outflank us.

ISAAC:
You don't have to say it twice.

Allison fires a round of shots but doesn't manage to hit anything. A woman runs at Jeremiah, he raises his shot gun and blasts the side of her head off.

JEREMIAH:
I am not ready for this.

JOHN:
Better get ready, quickly.

JEREMIAH:
What did these women do?

JOHN:
It's not what they did do, it's what they're going to do if they get to you.

The woman that Isaac missed gets close enough and engages him in hand to hand. Isaac pulls a knife and blocks a swing with her arm. The woman screams and Isaac slices his knife across her throat causing a thin red line to show.

ISAAC:
You're going to have to try harder than that.

ALLISON:
Isaac, watch out.

Isaac is suddenly jumped from behind by another woman. He struggles to try and free himself but is unable to. He tries to stab at her but she manages to wrestle the knife away and stabs Isaac in the neck with the knife. Isaac slumps to the ground.

ALLISON:
(screaming)
Isaac, no.

JOHN:
Shit, pull yourself together.

Rebecca starts to cry.

JEREMIAH:
C'mon Rebecca, we need you.

REBECCA:
This isn't what I signed on for.

JEREMIAH:
You're going to have to deal with it, we need you right now.

Lilith laughs. Jeremiah fires off a shot. A woman is hit but she doesn't go down but keeps walking.

JEREMIAH:
What the? They're immune to bullets now?

LILITH:
Do not doubt my power.

Rebecca fires her pistol and hits a woman. The woman drops. John goes to fire his gun again but is grabbed from the side by another woman.

JOHN:
Shit, where are they coming from?

JEREMIAH:
Stay there and I'll help you.

JOHN:
I don't need your help little man.

John tries to fight off the woman but she grabs him in a choke hold and holds him. John starts twitching but stops. Allison watches on in horror.

ALLISON:
No, John.

JEREMIAH:
Allison, we have to get out of here. They're more than a match for us.

Lilith is heard laughing again.

ALLISON:
Alright, everyone pull back.

JEREMIAH:
Don't have to tell me twice.

The three remaining inquisitors back up to the van with the women surrounding them. Allison gets in the van and Jeremiah and Rebecca jump in the side doors. The van starts up and Allison drives off between two of the women.

INT. - VAN – DAY

REBECCA:
(crying)
What now?

ALLISON:
(frustrated)
I don't know.

JEREMIAH:
We need to do something.

ALLISON:
I'm trying to think.

JEREMIAH:
Meet up with Joshua.

ALLISON:
What?

First Bride

JEREMIAH:
Head for Joshua's, he's our last hope.

ALLISON:
Right.

JEREMIAH:
That was part of our original plan anyway.

ALLISON:
Right.

JEREMIAH:
Are you okay?

ALLISON:
Yeah, it's just. I've known those two for a long time.

JEREMIAH:
We'll have time to mourn later, we have to regroup.

ALLISON:
You're right, it's just hard.

JEREMIAH:
Just try and stay focused. Rebecca, are you gonna be okay?

REBECCA:
I've never seen anyone get killed before.

JEREMIAH:
It'll take a bit of time, but you'll be okay.

REBECCA:
I don't know if I will be.

JEREMIAH:
You have to be, we need you.

REBECCA:
Okay, for you, I'll try.

JEREMIAH:
That's enough for me.

ALLISON:
That's kind of a mixed intention.

JEREMIAH:
I'll take whatever I can right now.

ALLISON:
Alright.

INSERT – OUTSIDE VIEW FROM WINDSHIELD

A view of a city is seen from the front window.

ALLISON (V.O.):
There's the city that Joshua's in. Hopefully we can regroup and get reinforcements there.

BACK TO VAN

JEREMIAH:
Okay, let's go then.

EXT. - VAN – DAY

The van drives down the road towards the city.

EXT. - FARMHOUSE LIVING ROOM – NIGHT

The living room of the house is perfectly set together and GEORGE and BETH are sitting down watching T.V.

GEORGE:
I think it was a little extreme

BETH:
What was?

GEORGE:
You freaking out and going and getting Bobby from his friends house.

BETH:
I was concerned about him.

GEORGE:
All he did was fall.

BETH:
He scratched his knee.

GEORGE:
He's a little boy, it happens.

BETH:
Not to my boy it doesn't.

GEORGE:
How do you expect him to toughen up if you keep treating him like a porcelain doll?

BETH:
Excuse me, but I love my son.

GEORGE:
I just think you try to protect him to much.

BETH:
Is it a sin to love my son too much?

GEORGE:
That's not what I'm saying.

BETH:
It sure sounds like it.

GEORGE:
You're overreacting again.

BETH:
Well why don't you go to your priest and tell him all about me.

GEORGE:
Not this again.

First Bride
BETH:
I just don't see the point in you and my son going to that church.

GEORGE:
You know that it's something that's important to me.

BETH:
I don't trust that place.

GEORGE:
Why?

BETH:
You hear all those stories about priests molesting children all the time and you have to ask me why?

GEORGE:
My priest is not a child molester.

BETH:
That's what all their brainwashed congregations say.

GEORGE:
I am not brainwashed.

BETH:
I disagree.

GEORGE:
Since when have I done anything like that?

BETH:
That fact that you still go to that ridiculous church is evidence enough.

GEORGE:
I love you and all, but this is ridiculous.

Lilith and women walk past the window, stop and look in.

BETH:
It's non ridiculous, I don't want my son being narrow minded like you.

GEORGE:
I am not narrow minded.

BETH:
You treat me very well and provide for me in all ways, but I don't like you indoctrinating my son.

GEORGE:
Oh give it up.

BETH:
I will not.

GEORGE:
Fine then, I'm going to bed.

BETH:
Fine, you do that.

GEORGE:
Good night.

George gets up and leaves the living room and can be heard going upstairs.

BETH:
Men.

Beth picks up a wineglass then goes upstairs as well.

INT. - UPSTAIRS HALLWAY – NIGHT

Beth walks up to the room that Bobby is sleeping in and looks in on him. She smiles as she looks at him.

EXT. - ROADWAY – NIGHT

Lilith raises her hand towards the farmhouse.

LILITH:
Come.

INT. - UPSTAIRS HALLWAY – NIGHT

Beth's mouth twitches as she watches Bobby. She shakes it off but her mouth twitches again.

EXT. - ROADWAY – NIGHT

LILITH:
Come.

INT. – UPSTAIRS HALLWAY – NIGHT

BETH:
I know what I have to do.

Beth walks over to the bedroom door and opens it up.

INT. - PARENTS BEDROOM – NIGHT

George is laying down trying to get some sleep. When the door opens he turns over and looks at Beth.

GEORGE:
I don't feel like arguing with you anymore.

BETH:
Then don't.

GEORGE:
What? That doesn't sound like you.

BETH:
That's because ...

GEORGE:
Because what?

BETH:
It's not.

GEORGE:
Huh?

First Bride

Beth jumps on top of George and begins to choke him. He tries to fight her off but she proves to be to strong. He starts trying to hit her to get her off but it isn't working.

GEORGE:
Please stop.

BETH:
Die now.

GEORGE:
Please, I love you.

Beth just glares down at him and watches as his eyes roll back into the back of his head. George's hands falls to his sides and he lays there, lifeless.

BETH:
I don't love you, not anymore.

INT. - UPSTAIRS HALLWAY – NIGHT

Beth walks out of the bedroom and into Bobby's room. She is seen carrying BOBBY in her arms as she comes out.

BOBBY:
Mommy, what's going on?

BETH:
Shhh, honey. All will be fine soon.

BOBBY:
I want to go back to sleep.

BETH:
Soon, son, soon.

Beth goes down the stair with Bobby.

EXT. - ROADWAY – NIGHT

Beth emerges from the house with a knife in her hand and walks up to Lilith. Lilith looks in anger at Bobby.

LILITH:
What is this?

BETH:
My mistress, it is my sacrifice to you.

Lilith smiles.

LILITH:
I accept your sacrifice.

Beth hands Bobby to Lilith. Lilith holds him out on his back. Beth raises the dagger and plunges it into Bobby.

EXT. - HILLTOP – NIGHT

Lilith and the women emerge on the hilltop with a view of the city below.

LILITH:
Our journey is almost up.

SUSAN:
Yes, mistress.

LILITH:
We have one more to retrieve and then we meet up with my lord. Come let us go.

The women start walking towards the city.

Act 4

EXT. - JOSHUA'S HOUSE – NIGHT

The van carrying the inquisitors pulls up to the curb since the driveway is full. The inquisitors come out of the van, Jeremiah stretches and Rebecca comes out apprehensively.

JEREMIAH:
This is?

ALLISON:
Yeah, we better get inside quickly.

JEREMIAH:
You think we're in that much danger?

ALLISON:
Wouldn't surprise me, not after what happened.

JEREMIAH:
Good point.

Allison walks up to the front door and rings the doorbell.

ANXIOUS INQUISITOR (V.O.):
Who is that?

JOSHUA (V.O.):
Just hang on, I'll go check.

REBECCA:
You'd think they don't trust us.

ALLISON:
Something must have happened.

REBECCA:
Like what?

ALLISON:
I don't know.

JOSHUA (V.O.):
Who is it?

ALLISON:
It's Allison.

JOSHUA (V.O.):
How can I know it's you?

ALLISON:
You were expecting me.

Joshua opens up the door and peeks out. After seeing who it is he opens the door.

JOSHUA:
It's really you.

ALLISON:
Who else would it be?

JOSHUA:
We've had some incidents while waiting.

ALLISON:
Like what?

JOSHUA:
Come in and I'll tell you ...
    (pause, looks at Jeremiah and Rebecca)
... who are they?

ALLISON:
This is Jeremiah and Rebecca, they're with me.

JOSHUA:
Are you sure?

ALLISON:
Umm, yeah.

JOSHUA:
Alright.

INT. - JOSHUA'S LIVING ROOM – NIGHT

Allison, Jeremiah and Rebecca walk into the house inside they see ANXIOUS INQUISITOR and four other men sitting in on the couch and chairs watching the news.

ALLISON:
Okay so what happened?

JOSHUA:
We've had a few visits by Samael's followers.

ALLISON:
Is everyone okay?

JOSHUA:
No, we've lost about four people.

ALLISON:
What did you do with the bodies?

JOSHUA:
Typical disposal.

ALLISON:
I see.

ANXIOUS INQUISITOR:
I don't trust them.

JOSHUA:
I've known Allison a long time, she's welcome here.

First Bride
ALLISON:
Thank you.

ANXIOUS INQUISITOR:
I still don't trust them.

JOSHUA:
Well, too bad.

ALLISON:
Have you been able to get any more information as to when they plan to meet up with Lilith?

JOSHUA:
No, I haven't. We've been keeping an eye on them though and they haven't moved lately.

JEREMIAH:
Hopefully they're not causing diversions.

JOSHUA:
We're prepared for that.

JEREMIAH:
If you say so.

JOSHUA:
I've been doing this a long time.

ALLISON:
C'mon, cut him some slack.

JEREMIAH:
Fine.

ALLISON:
How'd they find us?

JOSHUA:
I'm not sure.

ALLISON:
I'm sorry.

JOSHUA:
The costs of war I guess.

REBECCA:
That's kind of cold.

JOSHUA:
You become this way after awhile.

ALLISON:
Where can we get some rest.

JOSHUA:
I'll show you.

EXT. - POLICE STATION – NIGHT

Lilith and eight women stop in front of the police station. The women all turn and look at it. NERVOUS BYSTANDER walks by and picks up their pace as they walk by.

SUSAN:
Is our last sister here?

LILITH:
She is.

BETH:
What do you wish of us.

LILITH:
Keep these men off me and I will rescue the sister.

SUSAN:
Yes mistress.

They all walk into the police station.

INT. - POLICE STATION RECEPTION – NIGHT

The women walk into the reception area and BORED CONSTABLE stands up to greet them.

BORED CONSTABLE:
Hi, can I help you ladies?

Lilith smiles and the women start to circle around him.

BORED CONSTABLE:
Ladies, I'm not in the mood for this crap so please just state your business or leave.

The ladies start jumping over the desk. As they do so the Bored Constable pushes a panic button under the desk. The women grab onto him and start bashing his head against a wall. He pulls his gun but the women turn his head to mush.

LILITH:
We must act quickly, they will be here soon.

The women walk up to a door and try to open it but it is sealed shut. Lilith walks up and pulls the door of its' hinges with no effort. The women start flooding into the stairway behind it.

INT. - CELL BLOCK – NIGHT

CELL GUARD and PANICKED GUARD are waiting in the cell block when the first of the women start coming through the door. They have their service pistols drawn and are awaiting the women. Police Sergeant is yelling orders over the radio.

POLICE SERGEANT (V.O.):
All officers to the cell block, protect the prisoners.

CELL GUARD:
Hold it right there. Don't move.

LILITH:
Silly boy thinks he can stop me.

Cell Guard raises his service pistol.

LILITH:
Do it boy, see where it will get you.

Cell Guard shoots Lilith. Lilith's head goes back but she quickly stands back up straight and the bullet hole closes up.

CELL GUARD:
Holy shit.

LILITH:
Foolish child.

PANICKED GUARD:
Sorry man, I'm not dying for these swine, I'm outta here.

Panicked Guard runs up the stairs. Cell Guard points his gun at them again. The women ignore him and Lilith thrusts her hand into his chest and pulls out his heart. The Cell Guard falls to the floor dead.

SUSAN:
Which cell is she in?

LILITH:
The big one on the end.

SUSAN:
The drunk tank.

LILITH:
Yes.

The women walk down to the end of the cell block and Lilith approaches the bars. Hanna goes to the bars eagerly.

HANNA:
Mistress, I am here.

LILITH:
You have failed me.

HANNA:
It wasn't my fault. They wouldn't let me.

LILITH:
So men stopped you?

HANNA:
Yes, they did.

LILITH:
Very well then.

HANNA:
Do you forgive me?

LILITH:
I do not forgive, but you must do what I need you to do.

HANNA:
I'll do it, I swear.

LILITH:
Very well then.

Lilith reaches and rips open the cell door. Hanna comes out.

POLICE SERGEANT:
Freeze bitches.

Lilith looks at the him and smiles.

EXT. - POLICE STATION – NIGHT

Flashes in basement windows and screams can be heard. Shots of blood smear the windows. The violent sounds end and Lilith and the women emerge with Hanna and into the street.

SUSAN:
Now what mistress.

LILITH:
Now we go to him.

SUSAN:
The time has finally come.

LILITH:
Yes, the end is here.

INT. - JOSHUA'S HOUSE – NIGHT

The house is dark and people are sleeping. The lights suddenly turn on with a frantic Joshua running around.

JOSHUA:
Up, everyone up. It's time.

ANXIOUS INQUISITOR:
Dude, it's two in the morning.

JOSHUA:
I don't care, Lilith and Samael are on the move. It's time to go.

ANXIOUS INQUISITOR:
Oh shit.

ALLISON:
What did you say?

JOSHUA:
You heard me.

ALLISON:
Alright, let's get moving.

JEREMIAH:
Is there enough of us here?

JOSHUA:
What we have will have to do.

JEREMIAH:
You didn't see what happened last time.

JOSHUA:
Then start praying, this is the only chance we'll get.

EXT. - ABANDONED WAREHOUSE – NIGHT

The van and three black cars pull up to the abandoned warehouse there is an old church across the road. All the inquisitors get out. They go to the back of their respective vehicles and pull out their guns and body armor. Joshua and Allison walk up to a partially open door.

First Bride
JOSHUA:
I'll go first.

    The rest catch up with them.

ALLISON:
You sure?

JOSHUA:
I know the lay out, I can find cover quicker than anyone else.

ALLISON:
Alright, if you say so.

    Joshua opens the door and a MAN with his back turned is there. Joshua goes up behind him and jerks his head to the side, breaking his neck. The man slumps to the ground.

ALLISON:
Efficient.

JOSHUA:
Quite.

INT. - ABANDONED WAREHOUSE – NIGHT

    Joshua takes cover behind some old moldy crates. Light flickers in the middle of the room and Joshua peeks over to see what is going on. He has a look of shock and waves for the rest to follow him. Allison comes up behind him.

ALLISON:
What's going on?

JOSHUA:
You might want to see this.

    Allison takes a look over the crates and see SAMAEL naked, having sex with Lilith. FIVE MEN and the eight women all stand around them watching. Another CREATURE with a snarling face and gray textured body and wings is curled on the ground and growing.

ALLISON:
What is that?

JOSHUA:
Must be the army their trying to raise.

ALLISON:
How many do you figure there are?

    Lilith screams and Samael pulls away. Another CREATURE emerges from her womb and begins growing. The other one that was first seen stands and flies up into the rafters. Allison looks up and sees ten of the creatures flying around.

ALLISON:
This doesn't look good.

JOSHUA:
We can't pull out now.

ALLISON:
True.

Joshua signals the four inquisitors who are huddled further down the room. Jeremiah and Rebecca crouch behind the crates and ready their weapons.

JEREMIAH:
Hopefully we'll be home in time for breakfast.

ALLISON:
If we're home for breakfast.

JEREMIAH:
At least try and be positive.

ALLISON:
I am.

Jeremiah looks in shock at Allison. Joshua aims and takes a shot. One of the women standing around them falls. All the women and men turn and start running. The creatures flying above don't take notice yet.

ALLISON:
Everyone, open fire.

A firing line begins. Three of the women get shot. Susan, Beth and Hanna are still alive. Two of the men also get shot and fall. The men and women reach the crates and jump over them with little effort.

JOSHUA:
Dammit.

ALLISON:
Try and fight them off.

JOSHUA:
I know.

Joshua pulls a knife and stabs one of the men. Allison hits a woman right in the sternum and then hits her in the head with the butt of her gun. The woman drops with little effort.

JOSHUA:
That wasn't so bad.

A male scream is heard and they turn to see two of the four inquisitors dead. Rebecca is struggling with a woman and Jeremiah is stabbing another woman. The other inquisitor and Anxious Inquisitor back off and open fire on the remaining man who dies.

JOSHUA:
You had problems before?

JEREMIAH:
We were just lucky.

JOSHUA:
I don't believe in luck.

Lilith and Samael take notice as Hanna runs off.

SAMAEL:
Kill them my children.

The ten creatures flying from above descend down to the inquisitors. They start firing and one creature is taken down. Two of the creatures descend on the Anxious Inquisitor and the other inquisitor and rip them apart.

First Bride
    REBECCA:
This is not good.

    ALLISON:
Just shoot them.

    Joshua, Allison, Rebecca and Jeremiah fire at the two creatures and they are killed. Joshua is suddenly pulled from behind and his head is ripped from his body.

    ALLISON:
    (frantic)
Joshua, no.

    Allison shoots the creature who ambushed them from behind. Black blood sprays all over Allison. Allison points her gun up in the air and begins firing. Lilith and Samael start moving towards them.

    JEREMIAH:
Umm, Allison.

    ALLISON:
What?

    JEREMIAH:
We have bigger problems approaching us.

    Allison looks at Lilith and Samael coming towards them.

    ALLISON:
Oh shit.

    JEREMIAH:
You got that exorcism ready?

    ALLISON:
Yeah I do.

    Jeremiah shoots up into the air and two more creatures fall to the ground. A creature lands behind Rebecca in the shadows, unseen. He sneaks up Rebecca, grabs her and throws her to the other side of the room.

    JEREMIAH:
    (screaming)
Rebecca.

    Allison opens fire and kills another creature. Lilith and Samael walk up to the crates. Allison points her weapon at him.

    ALLISON:
    (in Latin)
By the authority of heaven, you are condemned and I command you back to the abyss.

    Samael screams. Lilith sees what is going on and screeches. Samael shakes off the screaming and impales Allison on his arm as he lifts her in the air.

    ALLISON:
    (coughing up blood, in Latin)
By the authority of heaven, I command you.

    Allison dies. Samael slumps to the ground lifeless. Jeremiah fires off a couple more shots and two more creatures fall from the sky. Jeremiah sees he has no chance and runs out of the warehouse.

EXT. - ABANDONED WAREHOUSE – NIGHT

Jeremiah sees the old church and runs for it.

JEREMIAH:
Please, work.

INT. - OLD CHURCH – NIGHT

Jeremiah comes through the doors of the church and looks around. He runs up to the altar and points his gun at the door and waits. The door blows open and closed. Then it opens and Hanna walks in.

JEREMIAH:
Hanna? What are you doing here?

HANNA:
I've come to save myself.

JEREMIAH:
What do you mean?

HANNA:
Why Lilith of course, she has saved me.

JEREMIAH:
You serve her? Are you crazy?

HANNA:
You left a void in my life, she filled it.

JEREMIAH:
But you left me.

HANNA:
Yes, but you caused the wound.

JEREMIAH:
I'm not taking blame for this.

Lilith sneaks in through a back door and comes up behind Jeremiah.

HANNA:
But it's all man's fault. You are to blame.

Lilith grabs Jeremiah from behind and begins to strangle him.

JEREMIAH:
No.

Jeremiah tries to kick Lilith but she doesn't let go.

REBECCA:
Hey bitch. Let him go.

Hanna spins around and Rebecca shoots her in the head. Hanna drops.

JEREMIAH:
(strangled)
Get out of here.

First Bride
>REBECCA:
>*(in Latin)*

Unclean spirit, by the power of holy mother Mary you are to go back to your prison.

>LILITH:

No, you have no power here.

>REBECCA:
>*(in Latin)*

Now.

>*Lilith drops Jeremiah and screams. Her eyes turn blood red then clear up. She collapses to the ground and the screaming dies out.*

>REBECCA:

Jeremiah, are you alright.

>*Jeremiah coughs.*

>JEREMIAH:

Yeah, thanks.

>REBECCA:

No problem.

>JEREMIAH

How'd you know the exorcism?

>REBECCA:

I found it on Allison's body and remembered it as I ran over here.

>JEREMIAH:

Thank you.

>*Rebecca smiles.*

>REBECCA:

What do you think they're going to say back in the Vatican?

>JEREMIAH:

I don't think they'll be happy.

EXT. - VATICAN CITY – DAY

>*A view of the Vatican is seen in the bright afternoon sky.*

>BISHOP MICAH (V.O.):

So you say Sister Allison was killed and you took the mission on your own?

INT. - VATICAN COUNCIL ROOM – DAY

>*Jeremiah is sitting in the middle of a room surrounded by BISHOP MICAH, BROTHER ANDREWS, BROTHER AARON and BISHOP PAUL.*

>JEREMIAH:

I believed everyone else was dead.

>BROTHER AARON:

Did it not occur to you to withdraw and call the Vatican.

>JEREMIAH:

I tried to get out of there.

BROTHER AARON:
You said you ran into the church.

JEREMIAH:
I was trying to pull myself together.

BISHOP MICAH:
What you did was foolish.

JEREMIAH:
It all worked out in the end.

BISHOP MICAH:
That is besides the point.

Jeremiah just lowers his head.

BISHOP MICAH:
According to your report you said Brother Andrews met you at Allison's house. Is that correct?

JEREMIAH:
Yes it is.

BISHOP MICAH:
He never left the Vatican.

JEREMIAH:
Yes, he did, he was at her house.

BISHOP MICAH:
Brother Andrews, were you at Allison's house?

BROTHER ANDREWS:
(hesitantly)
No I was not.

BISHOP MICAH:
What do you have to say to that?

JEREMIAH:
I guess I was wrong.

BISHOP MICAH:
And this claim that Lilith was once Adam's wife?

JEREMIAH:
That was information we stumbled upon from a credible source.

BISHOP MICAH:
And what was that source?

JEREMIAH:
I prefer not to say.

BISHOP PAUL:
In other words, Brother Andrews.

JEREMIAH:
It obviously wasn't him.

BISHOP PAUL:
Then why did you include this heresy?

First Bride
JEREMIAH:
I was reporting everything.

BISHOP PAUL:
Are you suggesting the church is wrong?

JEREMIAH:
I didn't say that.

BISHOP PAUL:
It is obvious you think so.

JEREMIAH:
I must have been wrong.

BISHOP MICAH:
I believe our minds are made up. Jeremiah you are relieved of your duties until we decide the honesty of your report and confessions. You may leave.

Jeremiah gets up and walks out of the room.

INT. - HOTEL ROOM – DAY

Jeremiah is looking out the patio door and Rebecca is laying naked and asleep on the bed. Jeremiah jumps when a knock is heard at the door. He opens the door and Brother Andrews is on the other side.

BROTHER ANDREWS:
May I come in?

JEREMIAH:
How'd you know I was here?

BROTHER ANDREWS:
We're the Inquisition, we know everything.

JEREMIAH:
Right.

Rebecca moans and looks at what's going on. She screams and covers herself up.

REBECCA:
What are you doing here?

JEREMIAH:
Yeah come in.

Brother Andrews walks into the room.

BROTHER ANDREWS:
I've come to tell you that you are re-established into the Inquisition. Congratulations, you can go back to work.

JEREMIAH:
Thanks, I guess.

BROTHER ANDREWS:
And I've come to apologize about my conduct at the hearing.

REBECCA:
Yeah, why did you deny being at the house?

BROTHER ANDREWS:
If I admitted to it, they would charge me with heresy.

JEREMIAH:
But the church should know about Lilith.

BROTHER ANDREWS:
Some do, most do not. They choose to be ignorant.

JEREMIAH:
I wish you had been honest.

BROTHER ANDREWS:
Yes well.

Silence.

BROTHER ANDREWS:
I've also come to give you offer the first chance for a new mission, and trust me, you're not going to believe this.

BLACK SCREEN

JEREMIAH (V.O.):
I'm listening.

END

www.ingramcontent.com/pod-product-compliance
Lightning Source LLC
Chambersburg PA
CBHW030347030726
47499CB00003B/939